Shy
Willow

cat min

LQ

LEVINE QUERIDO

MONTCLAIR | AMSTERDAM | NEW YORK

There was once a rabbit named

Willow

who lived in an abandoned mailbox.

Willow didn't like being outside very much.

BAM!!

She preferred being
inside, in her home
where it was cozy
and quiet…

… just the way
she liked it.

One day, a blue envelope fluttered into her home.

Someone must've thought
that the mailbox still
delivered letters.

Dear Moon,

It's my mom's birthday tomorrow and I was hoping, if you're not too busy... could you shine your biggest and brightest at midnight for her special day? It would make her very happy.

Yours truly,
Theo
(the purple house on Eris Street)

me →

here ↓

"What a thoughtful birthday gift!"
said Willow.

The letter had to be delivered to the moon…

… but how?

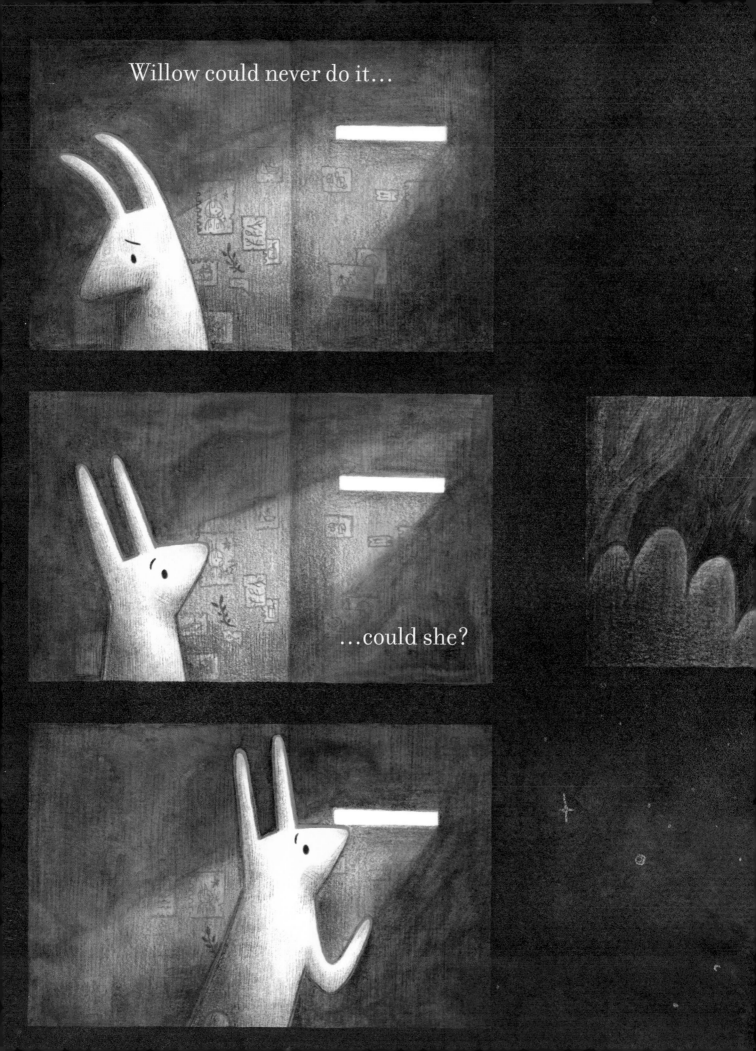

Thump, thump, thump!

Willow's heart beat faster.

As the sky dimmed, the moon slowly
shimmered into view. It was so, so
far away, and she couldn't scamper
back if she was scared.

It made her sad to think about Theo
and his mom waiting and staring at a
dark, empty sky.

If someone had to deliver the
letter to the moon by midnight,
she knew it had to be her.

Outside was big,
tall and scary.

Willow's knees
trembled as she
stared at the moon
in the sky.

Maybe if she
jumped high
enough, she
could reach the
moon.

She was a rabbit
after all…

...but the moon was too far away.

Willow wondered if she could climb her way up to the moon.

She found the tallest mountain and began to climb it.

Every time she
slipped, her
heart fell into her
stomach.

When she finally reached the top,
the moon was still far away.

It was getting darker. Willow longed to run
home. But she shook the thought away when she
remembered the little boy and his letter.

As Willow walked past a
tall tree, she heard baby
birds chirping in their nest above.

This gave her an idea.

Willow climbed up
a tall tree and hid
inside a nest.

She waited until a large bird flew past.

Willow jumped!

Willow held on tightly. She could
barely keep her eyes open.

The bird swayed, and a big gust of
wind blew towards them —

throwing Willow off the bird's back!

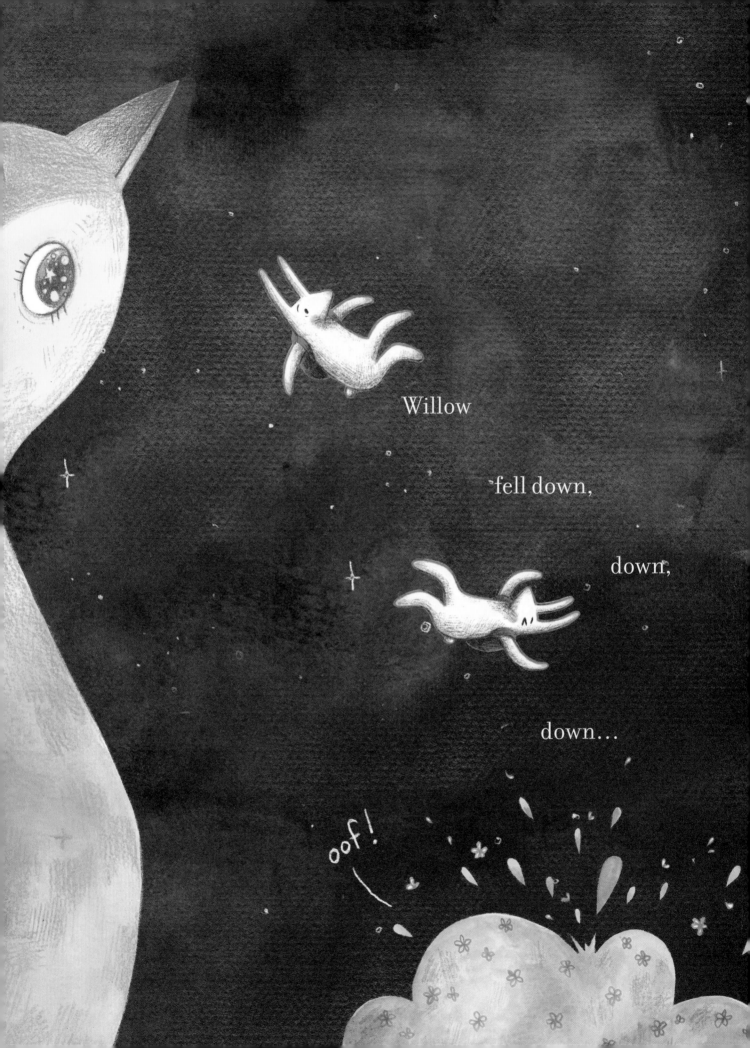

Willow

fell down,

down,

down...

oof!

Feeling lost and tired, Willow sat in a small
grass area surrounded by trees. It was
comfortable and reminded her of home.

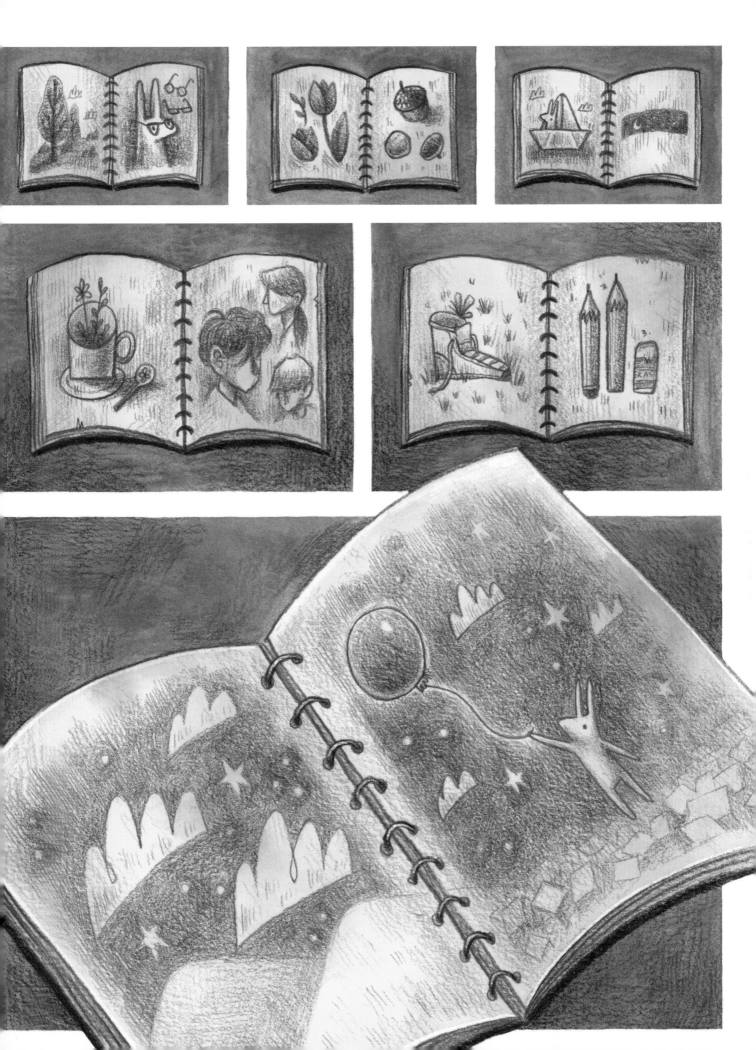

Out of all the things she did that night,
Willow took the biggest step yet.

When Willow finally arrived, the moon was sleeping.
Willow's heart beat faster than ever. Willow cleared
her throat and gently tapped the moon's cheek.

"Excuse me, ma'am,"
said Willow.

The moon stirred and slowly blinked
her eyes open. She yawned and turned
her gaze to Willow.

"Hello, I-I'm Willow. And this is for you."
She pulled out the letter from her backpack.

"A letter? For me? How lovely!" said the moon.

In a quivering voice, Willow read the letter to the moon.

"How brave of you to come all the way here to deliver this letter to me," said the moon.

"Midnight, is it? Well, then, we don't have much time.

Come along, Willow. This should be fun."

They glided through the sky.

And stopped just above Theo's house.

The moon set Willow down.

Willow gasped.

The warmth of the moonlight spread
through Willow's chest.

And it remained
there forever.

For my twin boys, KASTOR and POLLUX—my two rays of sunshine

This is an Arthur A. Levine book

Published by Levine Querido

LQ

LEVINE QUERIDO

www.levinequerido.com · info@levinequerido.com

Levine Querido is distributed by Chronicle Books LLC

Text and illustrations copyright © 2021 by Cat Min

Library of Congress Control Number: 2020937500

ISBN 978-1-64614-035-0

Printed and bound in China

Published in February 2021

First Printing

Cat Min created the art for this picture book starting with light
sketches on paper using an erasable pink colored pencil. She then
applied watercolor over the sketches, and once dry, used colored
pencils to add texture and detail. The illustrations were then
cleaned up and finalized digitally in Photoshop and Procreate.

Book design by Joy Chu

The text type was set in Filosofia OT